REMARKABLE
PEOPLE

Zac Efron

by Tom Riddolls
and Judy Wearing

Published by Weigl Publishers Inc.
350 5th Avenue, Suite 3304, PMB 6G
New York, NY 10118-0069

Website: www.weigl.com
Copyright ©2010 WEIGL PUBLISHERS INC.

All of the Internet URLs given in the book were valid at the time of publication. However, due to the dynamic nature of the Internet, some addresses may have changed, or sites may have ceased to exist since publication. While the author and publisher regret any inconvenience this may cause readers, no responsibility for any such changes can be accepted by either the author or the publisher.

Library of Congress Cataloging-in-Publication Data

Riddolls, Tom.
 Zac Efron / Tom Riddolls and Judy Wearing.
    p. cm. -- (Remarkable people)
 Includes index.
 ISBN 978-1-60596-628-1 (hard cover : alk. paper) -- ISBN 978-1-60596-629-8 (soft cover : alk. paper)
 1. Efron, Zac. 2. Actors--United States--Biography--Juvenile literature. I. Wearing, Judy. II. Title.
 PN2287.E395R53 2010
 791.4302'8092--dc22
 [B]
                                    2009005156

Printed in China
1 2 3 4 5 6 7 8 9 0 13 12 11 10 09

Editor: Heather C. Hudak
Design: Terry Paulhus

Photograph Credits
Weigl acknowledges Getty Images as the primary image supplier for this title. Unless otherwise noted, all images herein were obtained from Getty Images and its contributors.

Every reasonable effort has been made to trace ownership and to obtain permission to reprint copyright material. The publishers would be pleased to have any errors or omissions brought to their attention so that they may be corrected in subsequent printings.

Contents

Who Is Zac Efron?

Over the past few years, Zac Efron has become one of the best-known young stars in Hollywood. Zac first started his acting career in 1994 with an appearance on the TV show *ER*. Though he had small roles on many other shows, Zac reached stardom in 2006 when he appeared as the lead male character in Disney's TV movie *High School Musical*. Zac sang many of the songs on the movie **soundtrack** that became **hit** singles. In fact, he was the first new artist to have two songs debut on the *Billboard* Hot 100 at the same time. Another song from the soundtrack, a duet he sang with co-star Vanessa Anne Hudgens, moved from number 86 on the same chart to number four in just one week. At the time, no other song had ever jumped so many spots on the chart in such a short time. Almost overnight, people all over the world came to know Zac for his singing, dancing, and acting skills. After the success of *High School Musical*, Zac received many more offers for roles in big-screen movies. These **parts** often involve singing and dancing. For all his success, Zac still enjoys simple pleasures in life, such as hanging out with his friends and playing sports.

> *"I'm one lucky guy to have landed in such awesome projects."*

Growing Up

Zachary David Alexander Efron was born on October 18, 1987, in San Luis Obispo, California. Later, his family moved to a city called Arroyo Grande, 190 miles (306 kilometers) north of Los Angeles. Zac's father, David Efron, was an engineer who worked at a power plant. Zac's mother, Starla Baskett, had worked as a secretary at the same plant.

Growing up, Zac thought of himself as having an average life. Though he enjoyed having fun at school, Zac worked hard to earn good grades.

Zac and his younger brother, Dylan, were raised in a middle-income family. The brothers enjoyed playing sports, such as basketball, together. Zac liked to play sports, but his brother was a better athlete. At his father's urging, Zac began acting instead. He soon found that he enjoyed being on stage.

■ Zac calls himself a "regular dude."

Get to Know California

BIRD
Valley Quail

FLAG

FLOWER
Golden Poppy

0 ——— 200 Miles
0 ——— 200 Kilometers

California is the third-largest state in size. Only Alaska and Texas are larger.

The Pacific Ocean lines the east coast of California.

Many actors live in Hollywood. It is part of Los Angeles.

San Francisco is home to the Golden Gate Bridge.

California contains Mount Whitney, the highest mountain in the continental 48 states, and Death Valley, the lowest point in North America.

Think about it!

Acting is a job, and child actors must work, as well as do schoolwork. Often, child actors do not attend classes at schools. Instead, they have tutors to help them study. Child actors may spend long hours filming on movie and television sets, and attend special events. This takes a great deal of time. Think about the differences between your life and the life of an actor. What activities might you take part in that they do not? How are your lives the same?

Practice Makes Perfect

When Zac was 11 years old, he became interested in acting. He **auditioned** for a role in the musical *Gypsy* at the Pacific Conservatory of Performing Arts. He was chosen to play the part. From that time to the present, Zac has loved being on stage. He likes to hear people clapping and laughing for him.

Zac took classes at the Pacific Conservatory of Performing Arts. This community college in Santa Maria, California, trains actors and helps prepare them for careers in theater. Zac also began taking singing lessons and went to auditions every week. All the while, he continued to attend Arroyo Grande High School.

■ The musical *Gypsy* has been made into a movie and performed on stages across the nation, including on Broadway. Boyd Gaines, Laura Benanti, and Patti LuPone star in the Broadway show.

Zac landed roles in many school plays and worked with a theater company called The Great American Melodrama and Vaudeville. He also appeared on stage and in **commercials**.

The drama teacher at Zac's school knew he had talent. She asked a friend who was an agent to represent Zac's special skills as a singer and actor. The agent signed him to one of the best-known agencies in the sports and entertainment industries, Creative Artists Agency. This agency has represented some of the best-known actors and athletes in the world, such as Reese Witherspoon and David Beckham.

With the agent's help, by 2002, Zac had started landing small roles on TV shows, such as *ER*. Two years later, he took the part of Cameron Bale in a TV show called *Summerland*. At first, he was to appear in only a few shows. Soon, he joined the **cast** as a regular character.

■ On *Summerland*, Zac starred alongside Lori Loughlin and Jesse McCartney.

Key Events

Summerland was cancelled in 2005. Zac continued to get roles on other TV series, such as *CSI: Miami* and *The Suite Life of Zack and Cody*. An important step in Zac's career was landing a part as an **autistic** child in the TV movie *Miracle Run*. He was nominated for a Young Artist Award for his acting in this film. People began to take notice of the young actor.

In 2006, Zac's career took off. He was cast in Disney Channel's movie *High School Musical*. It was a surprise hit, and Zac gained instant stardom. More than 26 million people watched the movie the first few times it was shown on TV. A few months later, the movie soundtrack became the first soundtrack ever to reach the number one spot on the music charts.

The following summer, Zac made the leap from TV to big-screen movies. He appeared in the the musical *Hairspray*. His performance received good reviews, and people began to take Zac seriously as an actor. More acting jobs were offered to Zac.

■ To date, there have been two *High School Musical* movies on TV and one on the big screen.

Thoughts from Zac

Zac has worked hard to gain success as an actor. He feels lucky to land roles on TV shows and in movies. These are some of the things Zac has said about his career.

Zac talks about school and his *High School Musical* character, Troy Bolton.

"Personally, I was never the cool kid. I was always sort of a bookworm. I would just like to be more like Troy, because he's so cool."

Zac talks about being successful.

"If it happened to me, then, man, it can happen to anybody."

Zac talks about trying new things.

"You have to explore your boundaries and see where you really want to go and the only way you can do that is to break out of your shell."

Zac enjoys working with actors such as John Travolta.

"I love watching the guys who bring the cool into the story."

Zac knows he is just one of many actors in the business.

"Why did I get the parts I did? Who knows? But the minute I start thinking it's because I was special, that's when I know I'm in trouble."

Zac says that there is more to him than what appears in pictures.

"Photos are just a frame of your life; they don't represent what kind of a person you are."

What Is an Actor?

Actors are people that can pretend to be other people. They play characters in roles on TV, in movies, and in plays. Often, actors must learn lines and movements that are written in scripts. Sometimes, actors do not use a script. They say and do what they feel in the moment. This is called improvisation.

Good actors can cry on cue. When their characters are angry or upset, actors must show these feelings in a way that seems real. Some actors can change their voice or the way they look to seem like they are from another place or time. Costumes and makeup can help actors do this.

Some actors, such as Zac Efron, have other talents as well as acting. Zac uses his singing and dancing skills in many of his roles. Many of the movies he has worked on have been musicals. In these roles, he must act out his lines and show emotion while singing and dancing.

■ Actors, such as Zac Efron, often appear on TV talk shows to promote new movies.

Actors 101

Shirley Temple (1928–)

Shirley Jane Temple was a singing and dancing star at the age of six. Shirley was well known for her serious acting style and her curly hair. Many items, such as mugs, dolls, records, and dresses, were made with her **likeness**. Between 1936 and 1938, her movies made more money than any other actor. Shirley left Hollywood when she was a teenager. She traveled to other countries representing the United States.

Mary-Kate and Ashley Olsen (1986–)

Mary-Kate and Ashley Olsen are twins who were hired for their first acting job in 1987. The twins shared the role of Michelle Tanner on the TV show *Full House*. The show ended when the twins were eight years old. A few years later, the pair started their own movie **production company**. While they still act in movies, they also design clothes and home decor. Today, the twins are two of the richest women in show business.

Macaulay Culkin (1980–)

Macaulay started acting at the age of four. As a child, he went to acting school and ballet school. Macaulay has appeared in 17 movies, including *Home Alone*, *Uncle Buck*, and *Richie Rich*. Macaulay's dad was an actor who also managed Macaulay's career. Some people have said that Macaulay was the most successful child actor since Shirley Temple.

Miley Cyrus (1992–)

Miley Cyrus is best known for her role on TV's *Hannah Montana*. She is an actor, singer, musician, and songwriter. Miley's father is actor and country singer Billy Ray Cyrus. Miley grew up watching her father perform. She appeared with him on TV when she was nine years old. Five years later, she was chosen to be Hannah Montana. Miley has become one of the world's most influential teens. Zac Efron is one of her close friends.

Musicals

Musicals are movies, TV shows, or stage plays in which the actors have some spoken parts, but many of the words are sung. There are three main parts to a musical. These are music, **lyrics**, and a story. Dancing is often a part of musicals as well. Musicals are one of the oldest forms of entertainment. Today, many books and Hollywood movies are made into musicals.

Influences

Zac's parents worked hard to help Zac achieve his dreams. Zac's father, David, encouraged his son to try out for plays at his school. He also enrolled Zac in singing lessons. Zac's mother, Starla, would drive Zac to Hollywood a few days each week for auditions. Zac's parents were supportive of his career goals. They urged him to try his best, but they did not force him into the acting business.

John Travolta is one of Zac's favorite actors. John was born in 1954 in New Jersey. Like Zac, John can sing, dance, and act. John's first big screen success was in *Saturday Night Fever* in 1977. This is a movie about a young dancer. After starring in this movie, John was offered roles in movie musicals. One of his best-known roles was as the lead in the movie version of the Broadway musical *Grease*.

■ John Travolta played Danny Zuko in *Grease* alongside Olivia Newton-John, who played Sandy Olsen.

In 2007, John starred in a remake of the movie musical *Hairspray*. Zac also had a role in this movie. Zac has said that he was in awe of John on the film set. He was excited to work with one of his idols. After filming *Hairspray*, Zac said he learned a great deal about being a professional from working with John.

ZAC'S NEAREST AND DEAREST

Zac has two Australian shepherd dogs. Their names are Dreamer and Puppy. Zac also has a Siamese cat named Simon. Zac met his girlfriend, Vanessa Anne Hudgens, on the set of *High School Musical* in 2006. They have been a couple ever since. For her birthday in 2008, Zac bought Vanessa a house.

■ Zac and Vanessa often appear together at red carpet events or on TV talk shows.

Overcoming Obstacles

Whenother boys and girls his age were at school, Zac was trying out for roles in TV commercials and plays. He still had to do schoolwork so he would not fall behind other students. It was difficult for him to balance both acting and school.

At first, only a small number of Zac's auditions were successful. For every 30 to 40 auditions, Zac might land one part. Still, he was dedicated to his career, and he kept trying. He knew what he wanted in life and worked hard to make it happen.

■ Zac and some of the cast of *Hairspray* performed song and dance numbers on the *Today Show*.

Many of Zac's roles include dancing. Zac finds dancing a challenge and has to work hard to learn the moves. He practices at home and on set. Sometimes, other actors dancing in the same scenes spend extra time helping Zac.

After *High School Musical* was released, Zac became well known very quickly. People wanted to talk to or meet him. Zac's parents had to change their phone number because so many people called the house. It surprised Zac that so many people found him interesting.

■ People with cameras follow Zac wherever he goes, hoping to get an interview with him, or a picture of him to sell to tabloid magazines.

Achievements and Successes

After graduating from high school, Zac was accepted to the University of Southern California. He decided to wait to go to school. He wanted to focus on his career. Zac still plans to go to university in the future.

Disney's *High School Musical* was a surprise success. More than seven million people tuned in to watch its first airing. At the time, this was more than any other Disney Channel movie ever. In 2007, Disney produced *High School Musical 2*. More than 17 million people watched the first showing. This is the most ever for a Disney Channel movie to date. The next year, *High School Musical 3* was shown in movie theaters. In its first weekend, it made more money than any other movie musical in history.

■ Zac won the award for Choice Male Hottie at the 2007 Teen Choice Awards.

Though Zac's acting career has only just begun, he has had many achievements and succeses. The *High School Musical* movies have won many awards, but Zac also has been given many awards for his work on TV and in movies.

One of his first major roles, as Steven Morgan in *Miracle Run*, earned Zac a supporting actor nomination for the Young Artist Award for Best Performance in a TV Movie, Mini-series, or Special. Since then, he has had many other nominations and wins. Zac has won an MTV Movie Award, a Family Television Award, three Teen Choice Awards, and two Kids' Choice Awards. His role in *Hairspray* earned Zac a Young Hollywood Award in the category One to Watch. In 2008, Zac earned the number 92 spot on the *Forbes* 100 list. This list ranks the 100 most popular and promising celebrities every year.

HELPING OTHERS

Often, actors use their fame to help others. They may spread the word about non-profit organizations or help fund special causes. Zac lends his support to many different charitable organizations. In December 2008, Zac brought $10,000 worth of toys to children at Mattel Children's Hospital UCLA. He dressed as Santa Claus and spent time taking pictures with the children. Another time, Zac visited John Adams Middle School in Los Angeles on behalf of **DonorsChoose.org**. The non-profit organization helps fill classrooms across the United States with much-needed school supplies. One of Zac's favorite organizations is the Make-A-Wish Foundation. Children who are part of the Make-A-Wish group are often invited to visit the set of *High School Musical* movies to see them being filmed. To learn more about the Make-A-Wish Foundation, visit **www.wish.org**.

Write a Biography

A person's life story can be the subject of a book. This kind of book is called a biography. Biographies describe the lives of remarkable people, such as those who have achieved great success or have done important things to help others. These people may be alive today, or they may have lived many years ago. Reading a biography can help you learn more about a remarkable person.

At school, you might be asked to write a biography. First, decide who you want to write about. You can choose an actor, such as Zac Efron, or any other person you find interesting. Then, find out if your library has any books about this person. Learn as much as you can about him or her. Write down the key events in this person's life. What was this person's childhood like? What has he or she accomplished? What are his or her goals? What makes this person special or unusual?

A concept web is a useful research tool. Read the questions in the following concept web. Answer the questions in your notebook. Your answers will help you write your biography review.

- Where does this individual currently reside?
- Does he or she have a family?

- What did you learn from the books you read in your research?
- Would you suggest these books to others?
- Was anything missing from these books?

- Where and when was this person born?
- Describe his or her parents, siblings, and friends.
- Did this person grow up in unusual circumstances?

Your Opinion

Adulthood

Childhood

WRITING A BIOGRAPHY

Main Accomplishments

Help and Obstacles

Work and Preparation

- What is this person's life's work?
- Has he or she received awards or recognition for accomplishments?
- How have this person's accomplishments served others?

- What was this person's education?
- What was his or her work experience?
- How does this person work; what is or was the process he or she uses or used?

- Did this individual have a positive attitude?
- Did he or she receive help from others?
- Did this person have a mentor?
- Did this person face any hardships?
- If so, how were the hardships overcome?

Timeline

YEAR	ZAC EFRON	WORLD EVENTS
1987	Zac Efron is born.	Actress and singer Hilary Duff is born.
2002	Zac makes his first TV appearances on shows such as *ER* and *Firefly*.	*Spiderman* becomes the top movie of 2002, selling more theater tickets and DVDs than any other film.
2003	Zac acts in *Miracle Run* and is nominated for a Young Artist Award.	The top-selling album in the United States is *Get Rich or Die Tryin'* by 50 Cent.
2006	Zac graduates from high school.	*Hannah Montana* is first shown on TV in March.
2007	Zac stars in the movies *High School Musical 2* and *Hairspray*.	Forest Whitaker wins an Oscar for Best Actor for his role in *The Last King of Scotland*.
2008	Zac stars in *High School Musical 3* on the big screen.	*Shrek the Musical* is first performed on Broadway in New York City.
2009	Zac stars with Matthew Perry in the movie *17 Again*.	Kate Winslet wins the Golden Globe for Best Actress in a Motion Picture Drama for *Revolutionary Road*.

Further Research

How can I find out more about Zac Efron?

Most libraries have computers that connect to a database that contains information on books and articles about different subjects. You can input a key word and find material on the person, place, or thing you want to learn more about. The computer will provide you with a list of books in the library that contain information on the subject you searched for. Non-fiction books are arranged numerically, using their call number. Fiction books are organized alphabetically by the author's last name.

Websites

To learn more about Zac Efron, visit
www.zefron.com

To learn more about the *High School Musical* series, visit
http://tv.disney.go.com/disneychannel/originalmovies/
highschoolmusical

Words to Know

auditioned: performed to try to get a job in a movie or play

autistic: a condition in which a person has difficulty communicating with others

Billboard: a weekly magazine about music that tracks the popularity of songs

cast: all the actors in a musical or movie

commercials: short videos made to sell products

hit: a very popular movie or song that lots of people like

likeness: the quality of being like a certain person or object

lyrics: words that are sung in a song

musical: a play or movie with lots of singing

parts: characters in a movie or musical

production company: a company that pays for movies to be made

soundtrack: a collection of the music used in a movie or musical

Index